This book contains references to death and violence that may upset young readers.

OUT OF TOUCH, OUT OF TIME

Johnny Boneo

Out of Touch, Out of Time

Cover and illustrations by James Irwin Esparas

Published by:
Johnny Boneo
Philippines
pjboneo@gmail.com

First Edition
ISBN 978-62-10614-52-7

To those who are in a relationship,
who used to be in a relationship,
or just like love stories ...

May this resonate with you.

Chapter 1

Shake It Up Is All We Know

"Joey?" a voice calls out in a muffled whisper, "Joey? Joey!"

Down the middle row of the seats in the lecture hall, a young man's head is buried in his crossed arms on the table. He squints, looks around, and realizes he ended up sleeping in class. With a groan, he groggily blinks again at what's in front of him, scratching his curly black hair. It seems he hasn't gotten any sleep last night or so.

Beside him, a dark-skinned guy, who's the same age as him at twenty, with black hair styled in dreads and eyeglasses, is rocking him back and forth.

"Yeah, I'm awake," Joey mutters. "I'm awake now."

"You better be prepared for a recitation," Nico warns Joey in a British accent, rolling his eyes. "Professor Peterson's bound to call out random blokes, especially the sleeping ones."

"Mr. Barbossa!" the voice of Professor Peterson booms across the lecture hall, making Joey jolt up and stand.

"Yes, Professor?" asks Joey, gulping.

In his class, Professor Peterson likes to give out surprise recitations, so everyone must be prepared to answer.

"In our study of ethical frameworks," Professor Peterson says, "we've delved into the theory of utilitarianism, which proposes that the right action is the one that maximizes overall happiness or pleasure and minimizes suffering for the greatest number of people. Can you cite a real-life scenario where utilitarian principles are applied?"

Joey thinks for a while, gathering his thoughts for a real-life example of utilitarianism.

"Well, think about the, uh, ethical dilemma surrounding vaccination distribution during a pandemic," Joey replies, "with limited doses available, utilitarianism would prioritize high-risk groups, like, umm ... healthcare workers and the elderly, to save the most lives and minimize the spread of whatever sickness they may be battling with in that hypothetical situation."

"Excellent answer, Mr. Barbossa." Mr. Peterson gives out a small contented smile, nodding. "And with that, I believe we've covered enough ground for today. Class is dismissed."

With the class over, the students get off their seats and walk out of the doors; the noise of chatter and footsteps is heard.

Amid the emptying hall, Joey simply sits by the middle row, blankly staring at his iPhone screen with no notifications popping. He rolls his eyes, sighing and slouching back in frustration.

Something is bugging him, making him uneasy. He seems to be waiting for something to pop up; someone to text him back. But there is no response. He opens his contacts then hovers to the messages from a girl named "Lily". There are no new messages other than a dry "hi," "hello" and "how have you been" texts.

Just then, Nico shakes him back and forth for a while.

"Hey, Joey! You good, bruv? Lucky that you still got the answer right somehow."

Joey just looks at him, seeing the young man gaze at him funnily.

Nico must've noticed something as the other young man peers into his phone. "No new messages from Lily, eh?" he continues, nudging him.

"Yeah ..." Joey snorts with a forced smirk as he places his phone down onto the table. "I dunno what's even happening between her and me anymore."

"Wait, why?" Nico raises an eyebrow, pushing back his glasses.

"I know college life is complicated and how we're so busy and we gotta manage our time, studies, and other activities." The tanned young man then begins to rant, "Lately, we don't have enough time to be together."

"So that's what kept you up all night, huh? No wonder." Nico nods then asks, "I mean, I heard she's making lots of music and studying real hard, right?"

"Yeah," replies Joey, nodding. "Sure, we talk a little here and there, but it's ... dry. I don't know if we're gonna last long ..."

"Don't think like that, bruv!" Nico retorts, shaking his head. "You two are wonderful together. It's just the ups and downs of couples, so best to talk it out."

"You sure?"

"You could just be overthinking. You just need to hear her perspective. Besides, you seem like you don't hit her up much to begin with."

That sure shuts Joey up. Joey has indeed stopped texting Lily for a little while.

"It's hard for me to keep up the conversation if it's dry and she sounds uninterested," he explains, scratching the back of his neck.

"Still, bruv, communication is key."

"Alright," Joey nods in acknowledgment, now standing up with his stuff and shuffling off toward the lecture hall's exit, slinging his bag over his shoulder, "Off to lunch then!"

"Yup," Nico says with a grunt, stretching his arms out as he gets up to follow. "Wilbur's Dining?"

Wilbur's Dining is a restaurant that serves Filipino dishes.

"Why not?" Joey replies, agreeing. "Getting tired of buying those meal plans."

"I know, right? I wanna eat some adobo or dinuguan of yours again!" Nico exclaims.

Joey smiles at this, especially the mention of wanting to eat adobo—pork or chicken stew marinated in soy sauce, vinegar, and garlic—and dinuguan—pork stew with pig's blood and spices. The mere mention of these two dishes takes Joey and Nico back to their first meeting.

It was their first year at Stanford University and they were assigned as roommates in the shared apartment at Mirrielees House inside the campus. Joey cooked some "chocolate pork" and being the Filipino that he is, shared his favorite dish with his new friend. Surprisingly, Nico enjoyed it even when he found out later on what made the soup brown—pig's blood. This started a tradition of sorts of them eating Filipino dishes from time to time, if they have a stock of rice.

Joey laughs. "Next time for sure. Searched far and wide but there's no rice to buy anywhere, dude."

"Without rice, without them good Filipino foods," Nico sighs. "Geez."

"Exactly, Nico." Joey nods along. "Exactly."

With that, both walk out of the building, head to the parking lot which is a pretty short walk. The car is just parked near the Stanford Memorial Church.

"Hey, do you think Lily is cheating on me?" Joey asks.

"What? Heck nah, she isn't and she won't!" Nico's eyes widen and he shakes his head.

"How about her cheating with yo-"

"Don't even start. I've known her since we were kids and ever since you came to her life, she has always been talking about you when she hits me up." Nico's eyes dart wide open toward Joey's, upset that his friend would think that of his childhood friend. "I'm telling you, she absolutely adores you."

"Whatever you say, man."

"I'm serious! This is why you shouldn't mess this one up, got it?" Nico shouts out, patting his friend's head and leaning his ear close to hear his friend's reply.

Joey just smiles at this, walking up to the car. "Got it, man," he says as he now reels back from Nico, heading to the driver's seat of the white Toyota Camry.

He drives with Nico in the passenger seat. He makes a sign of the cross as they pass by a church.

In her side of the room filled with rock band posters, Lily sits by her computer setup, with a guitar cradled in her arms as she plays. The girl, sporting messily tied-up blonde hair and a black Nirvana T-shirt, is figuring out what notes will fit well by looking into the computer screen. She has some music-making software on, recording the guitar strings that she is strumming. While she plays the guitar, trying to figure out the perfect notes to fit in her upcoming song, her mind wanders off.

She can't shake off the thoughts about her boyfriend and how things have been changing. They still talk, yes, but there are times when they'd be talking, but it's like something is amiss, and then times when they don't talk at all. And in between, things have been dull between them. She can't help thinking, did she do something wrong? What even went wrong between them? She remembers the time when they were in their freshman year, confessing to each other how they'll make it work even if they're already in college. Three years later, here they are and it seems like they're not connecting lately. She wants to feel like it's all on her boyfriend, but at the same time, she feels as if she's the one at fault.

Lily stops her reverie when a knock is heard at the door. At that moment, she hopes it's Joey, coming over to talk it out. Watching as her roommate Jessica opens the door, she sees someone else. It's a guy with black hair and a big physique. Not Joey.

"Oh, bestie!" Jessica chirps. "Me and Tyler are gonna go out tonight, okay?" She tells Lily and heads out, forgetting to close the door.

Lily manages a forced smile, her disappointment masked by polite courtesy. "Have fun, you two," she replies, trying to sound sincere as she is left alone.

She sighs in her loneliness. As she goes to close the door, she sees a familiar person walking to her doorstep. The curly black hair, tan skin, and dark brown eyes ... that is Joey.

"Oh, Joey," she calls out softly. "Hey."

"Hey there!" Joey greets back, nervously chuckling as he scratches his hair. "Jess dating a new guy?"

"Her ex."

"Which one?"

Jessica has A LOT of exes for a sorority girl.

"Tyler, the big guy."

"Ah ... right."

Lily then crosses her arms. "So what got you here?"

"Well, uh," he stammers, but proceeds to show what's behind his back and hands a bouquet of lilies. "For you, babe."

Lily giggles. "Lilies again?"

"They remind me of you." Joey sheepishly grins, but realizes why he was here—to apologize. "Look, I'm ... worried about us ... Are we okay?"

Lily clicks her tongue, looking down at the floor, then up to Joey's brown eyes. "Joey, we're okay-"

"Are you really?" Joey interrupts, walking up closer to her. "I know I've been busy and so are you, and I'm sorry if you've been bored with me lately. Or I was making things boring ... I mean ..."

"No, no, no." She shakes her head. "I should be sorry. I got caught up with my studies too."

"I guess we forgive each other, then?" Joey looks to see her blue eyes. "I want us to talk more. I don't wanna lose you ..."

Lily just smiles, putting her right hand on his cheek and lightly slaps him. Joey can feel her soft palm caress his cheek. It tickles—it tickles and it is the best thing ever for him—making him smile.

"What are you saying? It's okay now, really ... especially with you here," Lily reassures him with a light peck on the lips, causing Joey to blush.

"So, what about a date to, uh, make it all up to you?" He has his hand on hers as her hand is still on his face.

"What?" Lily is astonished at this proposal, putting her hand out forward as she backs up. "Stay."

"I ain't no dog," he chuckles, though he stays to wait nonetheless as Lily rushes back inside to change.

When she comes out of her room, she is fully dressed in Joey's blue hoodie that looks a little too big on her, black leggings, black boots, a brown second-hand handbag, and her blonde hair flowing lusciously.

"Are we ... good to go now?" she asks, putting her right hand on her hip and grinning like a happy tiny elf with a bag.

Joey can't answer out of awe. She isn't one to spend so much time on makeup and styling her hair and clothes like other girls. She dresses up minimalistically and yet she's beautiful beyond words. At least that's how he sees her. Sometimes, he wonders just how he caught the attention of a girl like her.

"Hello-!" Lily waves at his face, snapping her fingers at him. "You there, pookie bear?"

"Oh, huh!" Joey snaps out of it and laughs at his new nickname. "And who are you calling a pookie bear now, little miss?"

Lily bursts into laughter because of Joey's shocked expression, now having a cheshire smug as she gives him a peck.

"YOU, pookie bear," she says, giggling and teasing him more.

All Joey can do is smirk as he looks at her with adoration, like Charlie from *Willy Wonka and the Chocolate Factory* winning a golden ticket.

"Whatever, let's go," he says.

With a smile, Joey holds her hand and they head to his car and off to their date.

Chapter 2

Using Bodies Up As We Go

Oh how fun it is driving down the street, heading for their date! Joey drives his secondhand white car while Lily sits beside him in the passenger seat as the radio plays their next song in queue. She recognizes "Out of Touch" by Hall and Oates after a few notes and shakes her head to the beat.

"Oh, I love this song!" the music major exclaims as she begins to sing along. Her voice is gracious, smooth like butter; it tickles Joey's ears just listening to her. She sounds like an angel. She raises her voice but keeps it in tone, nothing crazy.

By the time the first chorus rolls around, Joey chimes in for a duet. His voice is not horrible and not outstanding, yet passionate and going all out. Together, their voices blend well as two talented singers. They continue this as they drive up to Town & Country Village, a shopping plaza near Stanford University.

Singing along, the two lovebirds catch glances. Joey puts his eyes back on the road and sees all parking spots of the mall filled.

"Aw, man," he mutters as he now drives up to the parking lot on the other side of the road beside Town & Country.

That's okay. We just need to cross the street, he thought. Luckily, he secures a spot and parks near the exit.

"We're here!" says Joey as he unbuckles his seatbelt.

"Awww, we didn't get to finish the entire song," Lily pouts.

"Later, we'll do, baby," he replies reassuringly, kissing her forehead before getting out of the car.

Such a gentleman he is, Joey walks around the car to open and close the door for her. He holds her hand as they cross the street to get to the hacienda-style mall.

As they get to the other side, Joey notices not just how pleasantly cold this winter afternoon is, but also how crowded Town & Country Village has gotten today: the many cars filling up the parking lot and the many people walking around, shopping in stores and eating al fresco. Each one of these gives it all away. It surely isn't Valentine's Day, it's only January 17 today. He's glad they're together.

"Really would love to buy some clothes right now," mutters Lily as they pass by stores and stalls.

"Oh yeah?" Joey raises his eyebrow at this.

"Just feeling like getting new clothes, y'know?"

Joey replies, "That's it?"

"And that I want to look nicer to you."

"You don't have to do that!" Joey exclaims, going from just holding hands to wrapping his arm around her neck, tugging her close. "You look just as beautiful, Lily."

She giggles and blushes, snuggling close to her boyfriend. "Thank you, really."

"No problemo," replies Joey as he kisses the top of her head. "So which store are we going to?"

"That's the thing: I'm not sure ..."

The couple look around for clothing stores. After a minute or so, they finally find three stores for women side by side. All they have to do is pick which one to shop from.

"We goin' in here?" Joey asks as he points at the clothing store that says "Rutin" on the sign.

"Nope. Too fancy for me." She shakes her head in disapproval, then squinting at something as she looks at the window. "Also, why are there berries and nuts on display?"

Here's the thing about Lily: she isn't the type to dress up. She likes to and keeps it simple but if she does get into the mood of dressing up, she gets really picky.

"How about this one?" asks Joey, now pointing at the entrance of "Margaret O'Brien".

"I can tell by the name itself that those outfits are gonna make me look like a grandma." Lily looks at the clothes display and adds, "No offense but nah uh."

Joey chuckles at her comment as he walks up to the entrance of Evereve. "Hope this is the one," he murmurs as he points at the store.

Lily peers inside then turns to her boyfriend with a thumbs up and a toothy grin showing her pearly whites. "This is perfect, let's go!"

The blonde girl now holds Joey's hand tightly, dragging him along inside the white and gray interior. The smell of fresh, clean fabrics and the blasting cool air of the air conditioner caresses their face and skin as they enter.

He couldn't believe his eyes! There is a whole variety of styles of clothes to choose from—from casual to formal to a typical outing. It's probably because he is just so used to shopping at thrift shops.

With Joey trailing behind, Lily goes around the shop to get sweaters, shorts, dresses, and the like for her to try on. She checks herself in the huge mirror with the dresses and shirts to see if they look good on her. After that, with a huge bunch of clothes, shoes, and accessories, she hurries inside the changing room.

"Just stay right there." Lily closes off the curtains.

"Of course." Joey nods, putting his hands in his pockets and waits.

After a while, Lily comes out with the first outfit. She wears a blue v-neck t-shirt and bleached loose fit jeans, paired with white sneakers.

"How do I look?" she asks as she twirls around to show herself off to Joey.

"Simple and pretty." He beams at her, observing every inch of the outfit. "Fits you well and goes along with anything ... maybe even add a jacket to top it when it gets really cold outside."

"Not gonna lie." She looks down for a moment to check herself. "I'm getting pretty tired of going out in my old pants and leggings."

"Whatever floats your boat!"

Then Lily goes back inside, closing the curtains. About five minutes later, she comes back out with a white button-up collared shirt, a black leather jacket on top, along with a denim skirt and high-heeled boots.

"Babe, do I look fat in this one?" asks Lily, looking at herself.

"Never thought of you as a skirt kinda gal," Joey comments, smiling at her next outfit. "Looking amazing though."

"First time for everything, right?" says Lily as she tucks a strand of blonde hair behind her ear with a smile, then her smile drops as she stares dead into his eyes. "Seriously, answer the question."

"No, you look perfect in that one," he finally answers. "Must be painful walking around because ... you look like you fell from heaven."

Lily, taken aback by his line, blushes madly like a steaming tomato. His pick-up line sure is effective, even if deep down, Joey finds it pretty corny.

"Oh please!" exclaims Lily, giggling.

"As if I wasn't this smooth before." He chuckles with a smug look on his face.

"No, you weren't."

"Oh yes, I was."

"No, you weren't, Joey."

"How about you go try out the next outfit and find out?"

"I sure will."

Walking back to the changing room, loud rumblings are heard. They look at each other's stomachs, then toward each other's eyes; there is silence right before they burst into laughter. It's funny how they get along so well that even their stomachs are synchronized.

"Good thing that's my last outfit."

"Oh, okay. So, shall we?" He goes to her and leans in to kiss her on the cheek.

"Mhm." She nods and goes back to the changing room. "Just let me get back to my clothes, yeah?"

Joey nods as she closes the curtains to get dressed back into her hoodie, leggings, and boots.

Back in her own clothes, they head to the counter to pay for her new clothes and head out with shopping bags which Joey offers to carry.

"Which place to eat?" Lily wonders aloud, her arms wrapped around Joey's left arm.

"You down for some Mexican food?" Joey asks.

"Now that you mention that, man, am I craving some!"

"Mexican food it is then."

The couple head to Lulu's, a Mexican restaurant they passed by when they were looking for clothing stores. Luckily, there's only one customer waiting in line and four people eating outside since there are no indoor tables.

The smell of burritos, nachos, and the like, even seeing people eating them and savoring each bite is getting the couple impatient to get their food. Eventually, it is their turn to order.

"Can I get, uh, one Chicken Fajita Plate with corn tortillas, no beans, and brown rice, please? Then, uh ..." Joey says to the cashier then glances over to Lily, hoping she'd tell her what she wants.

"Anything," she replies softly, still holding herself close to him.

"They don't serve a plate of 'anything' here, sweetheart." Joey teases in a whisper, which Lily greets back with a slap to his arm.

"Ow."

He doesn't even find it painful, just ticklish. "But seriously, anything, really?"

"Mhmm," she nods.

"Alright, umm ... a Beef Fajita Plate with flour tortillas, whole pinto beans, and vegetarian cilantro rice."

As the young blonde cashier encodes their order by the cash register, she asks, "Any drinks?"

"Just water," Joey quickly answers and he pulls out his wallet to pay.

Lily just paid for her new clothes, so he's paying for their food. After ordering, they sit at the outdoor metal table near the glass door. All they have to do now is wait.

"Are you sure about paying?" Lily asks.

"Of course," Joey nods with an upside down smile, "I saved too much money, not exactly broke."

"Why did you look so worried about the price of my clothes, then?"

"Yeah, you got me ..." Joey grimaces, scratching the back of his head.

"Why be so frugal when your family's pretty rich? I mean, I know you guys barely got money in the Philippines back then, but now, you got a rich stepdad kind enough to send you to Stanford, Joey!" Lily continues, "Mirrielees literally costs over $5,000 and you get to live there with Nico!"

As he processes her question, Joey simply shrugs at this. "I guess I'm used to being so conservative with my money, if that even makes sense," he replies.

"But at least, let loose. Get a little more expensive, maybe? To treat yourself ... to treat us even?"

"Are you implying a fancy date next time?" Joey asks, raising an eyebrow.

"I'd love to but it's ... more than that." Lily chuckles slightly, "Life is temporary. You being oh so frugal is your way of being careful, I know, but best not be too careful. You might miss out on important things."

Joey ponders on her words. Being rich herself, he first interprets it as her trying to get him to spend more. However, it feels like she also wants to say that he's too tough on himself.

"See, this is why I fell for you, Lilian." Joey smiles, resting his chin on his hand as he gazes at her.

"Not you being cheesy again!" Lily laughs.

Joey chuckles along, smiling as he looks around. Their order isn't there yet.

"Hey, while we wait for our food, care to tell what you're up to lately?" he says, leaning close with his chin still resting on his palm.

"I know, right? The food better be good." She sighs, then continues, "so, uh, yesterday, a marketing executive came up to me and invited me to go make demo tapes."

"Just like how Justin Bieber got famous?" Joey asks, intrigued.

"Yeah!" She nods, beaming at him. "He saw one of my covers on TikTok and even told me I could get a record label, a manager even!"

Joey just grins as he sees how she's getting hyped up. He can tell she is very excited at this opportunity.

"My big break's soon, Joey!" She looks dreamy. "My course in music will pay off, as eventually, I'll be featured in songs, go to concerts, and get myself to write songs!"

"Holy–congrats, Lily!" He is excited for her too. "But you're not moving to where their studio is yet, right?"

"Staying for a while before I go, yeah ... and that is why I was busy."

"You should've told me more about it when we were texting." Joey playfully pouts.

"C'mon, it's supposed to be a surprise!" she says reassuringly, putting her hand over her lover's.

"So what have you been up to earlier this day?"

"Was working on a demo of this song I'm writing. Hold on, let me get my phone." She searches her handbag for her phone and earphones. "There it is!"

Lily then plugs the earphones in, handing over the right bud to Joey while she gets the left one. She swipes through her phone, looking for the song. Finally, she finds it and the music begins, with Joey closing his eyes to immerse himself in her music.

Chapter 3

Colors We Used to See

As the first few chords start, the tune gets a hold on Joey. The music is slow and sad, with a haunting melody that appears to be a sad soul's lament.

Joey closes his eyes, allowing the raw emotion of the music to sweep him away as the world around them fades into the background. Lily's voice is full of emotion as it bears the weight of the words she wrote. The lyrics talk about someone who feels undeserving of their lover. A genuine love confession filled with doubts and insecurities.

Joey asks, "Is this–"

"Shhhh!!!"

As Joey is shushed, he is now content, just engrossed in the song.

Lulled by the melody, he finds the lyrics so relatable. It reminds him of how she is the living definition of a hopeless romantic, wanting to be drawn to someone and fall in love like in the movies. The music resonates with him too, since he feels the same insecurities when it comes to love. He never planned to have a girlfriend. Before meeting Lily, he was adamant on purely focusing on his studies.

Just then, the unfinished demo abruptly stops.

Lily plucks out the earbuds from their ears. "So how's the song?" she sheepishly asks.

Joey gives her an outburst of clapping, with Lily giggling at his reaction.

"I'm just ... astonished at how you pulled off such a phenomenal song," comments Joey in a sophisticated, gentlemanly manner.

"Oh, stop!" Lily exclaims, wiping her tears of laughter. "But could you guess my inspo?"

"About you falling in love with me before we got together?"

"Bingo! That's the magic of listening closely to the lyrics!"

As they discuss the song, the waiter comes with their order: one Chicken and one Beef Fajita Plate with bottles of water, placed onto their table.

"Thank you so much!" Lily tells the server to which the server nods and smiles in response. They both open the styrofoam containers, revealing their dinner. Joey first prays for the food. Lily is about to take a picture but follows along with the prayer. Then, they both dig in.

Joey gets his plastic fork, taking a bite of chicken mixed with bell peppers and onions. He scoops a spoonful of brown rice as well ... and oh boy, is it delicious! The savory flavors are really going well with the chewy meat and the crunchiness of the bell peppers. He adds tortillas in them for even more chewy goodness in his mouth.

"Worth the wait, oh my!" Joey sighs with satisfaction while chewing his food.

Lily covers her mouth first as she chews, swallowing before speaking. "It's just alright ... around seven out of ten," comments the blonde girl.

"Not much your type?"

"It is my type, just not the best of the best. Also, whoever finishes their food last owes fifty bucks!"

Joey's eyes widen, but he smirks and accepts the challenge.

They race to finish their food first, even if it means stuffing their mouths like little hungry kids. Eventually, Lily stops eating, handing Joey her meal.

"I'm full, could you have this?" she pleads, pouting with puppy eyes. The plate had one fourth of food left.

"What?"

"I can't finish everything ..."

Sighing, Joey takes her plate and eats her Beef Fajita. As soon as he gulps the last bite, she laughs hysterically.

"HAHAHAHA! I WIN! Now you owe me fifty!"

"That's cheating!" Joey realizes he has been tricked and makes a face.

"No, really! It really got me full, babe."

He goes back to his plate and finishes everything quite quickly. As soon as he cleans his plate, he drinks his water.

"Can we go now?" Lily asks. "I have a group project tomorrow and I gotta get up early."

"Sure," he answers, then pauses to chug down some more water. "Not that we can do much around here." He nods as he closes the bottle.

With that, they take their bags and go down the sidewalk with Joey closer to the street. He is still drinking water. As soon as he spots a trash can, he throws his bottle. They then proceed to cross the road, waiting for the pedestrian traffic lights to go green before stepping forward. As the lights go green, he crosses the pedestrian near the intersection with his girlfriend, making sure she is close to him.

Everything is going good so far, he muses. His girlfriend is wrapped around his arm, close to him, and they're on their way back to the car, ready to head back home until ...

BEEEEP! BEEEEEP! SCREEEEEEECH!

Joey glances left and right confused with the barrage of noise. Just then, he realizes that a delivery truck doesn't seem to have working brakes and is about to crash into anything in its path. Anything and anyone.

Just when Joey is about to get run over by the truck, Lily shoves him to the side of the road, to safety. Desperately, Joey reaches his hand out to save her too. But it is too late. The truck crashes onto the blonde girl, and she rolls over right under.

"Liiiiilllllyyyyy!"

His voice and eyes are filled with horror, seeing Lily's body limp on the ground. Lifeless. Just then, all became quiet. All noise muffled. Joey can't hear anything. From the car alarms blaring, the ambulance siren whirring, to the passersby shrieking, panicking, calling 911.

Joey crawls to Lily, crawls because he can't seem to get up; his legs weak, his hands trembling.

This can't be happening. Everything is going so well. Surely, she's okay. It's probably just a broken bone. She's still alive, right?

Right?

Joey sits on a bench outside the trauma room of the hospital, his hands clasped as he murmurs prayers asking God to save Lily and hoping she is alright. From the Our Father, the Hail Mary, and the Glory Be, he whispers each and every prayer he can think of because he is panicking. He finds it difficult to breathe. His heart is beating so fast ...

There is no way she'd go like that. Lily is one of the bravest and strongest women I've ever met. She can hold her own. Why does she have to go like that? No, she will make it through. As far as I can remember, she never got sick or injured that often. I know she will recover and the truck that hit gave her nothing more than a headache ... Hopefully.

These thoughts linger in his mind as he tries hard to fill his mind with positivity, as he tries to fight the dread and fear that are eating him up inside.

Eventually, a male doctor with short black hair steps out of the trauma room and walks to Joey.

"Hey, Doc–" Joey speaks up, "is everything alright? Is she alright?"

The young doctor remains silent for a while, a pensive look on his face.

The silence is loud.

There is bad news coming.

But Joey refuses to give in to negativity.

"Doc, she's gonna be okay, right?" he asks, frantic, and holds the doctor's arm. "Coma? Maybe she's in a coma right now? But that's okay, she's gonna be back up again. That's the case, right?"

"I'm sorry, Sir, but ..." the doctor hangs his head low, unable to speak, then looks into Joey's eyes. "She didn't make it."

"Wha–" Joey whispers, full of distress and denial. "Wait–"

"I'm ... really sorry for your loss."

That is all the doctor can say, patting the young man's shoulder before breaking off from his grasp. Joey let his arms flop down, dangling as he tries to steady his breath and let the information sink in.

He then hears heavy footsteps and clattering from someone on heels walking down the ceramic white floor. He looks over and his eyes widen.

He sees a tall and muscular man-way bigger than Joey himself-with short blonde hair, dressed in a dark blue polo shirt, gray chino pants, and black loafers, alongside aviators obscuring his eyes.

Walking alongside him is a woman with a slender figure, light brown hair with a few gray and white streaks and eyes as blue as Lily's. She wears a purple silk dress with a gray blazer, probably from the tall man, draped over her shoulders, and circular glasses.

These are Lily's parents. The dad has a scowl on his face, eyes dart at Joey, as if he's going to kill someone—him. Meanwhile, his wife looks worried, getting in the giant of a man's way before he does anything drastic. But Joey does nothing, except to look away and look down in shame.

"Honey, stop-" the mother pleads, blocking the big man, but is lightly shoved aside.

"You-" The father aims at Joey as he delivers a right hook toward the young man's jaw, causing him to stagger to the floor.

Joey says nothing, he feels nothing, his eyes looking down. His body is numbed by the news. Nothing is more painful than Lily's demise.

"Stop it!" the mom screams.

But the dad isn't done yet. He grabs the younger man by the collar with his left hand, lands another punch. A staff member in the hospital steps in and breaks them off. But it isn't easy. This is not a fight. Only the older one is throwing punches, the younger is just receiving them.

"I trusted you, Joey! I trusted you when my baby texted me saying you two were going on a date!" the older man yells at Joey's face as he grabs his collar with both hands, fueled by a father's rage. "BUT LOOK WHAT HAPPENED! YOU WERE SUPPOSED TO PROTECT HER WHEN I'M NOT AROUND!"

Lily's mom is crying on the side. "Stop him, please."

But the hospital staff member is pushed back.

Violence is no solution to anything but the old man has a point. Why didn't he step in to save Lily when they're about to be hit by a truck? He is supposed to be a man—a man willing and capable to defend his loved one.

Many have done so much for him—his mother who took care of him; his stepdad lifting him and his mom from poverty; Nico, his first friend when he moved to America; and Lily, a supportive and loving girlfriend. He tried his best to pay back their kindness but he couldn't even protect his girl from a crazy truck. Why does he deserve such loving people when he can't keep his one true love safe?

"Are you even gonna say something? Are you even this heartless!" the old man continues yelling. "SAY SOMETHING!"

"Alright, that's enough!" Nico arrives to break the two apart, dragging Joey away from the dad as the hospital staff member holds Lily's father.

"Stay out of this, Nico!" Lily's dad yells, fuming yet trying to keep his cool toward the other boy.

"Not until you stay away from my best friend over here," Nico replies, helping Joey get back on his feet. "Seriously, let's calm down and stop fighting."

"You're telling ME to calm down?" The father grits his teeth.

Joey knows that Nico and Lily grew up together in San Francisco. Nico's British-American family and Lily's American family are friends. Thus, seeing Mr. Forester threaten his friend's son is bewildering to Joey. The old man must be so mad, and why not when he has just lost a daughter?

"You're right, Mr. Forester. I messed up." Joey speaks up, distancing himself from Nico as he regains his balance to stand on his own. "I didn't do anything when she pushed me out of the way. I'm an idiot-"

"Joey-" Nico tries to calm him down, attempting to pat his friend's shoulder, but Joey swats his arm away. "I'm just gonna be a sobbing mess if I just stay here longer, asking for an apology ... and I may as well give you so many sorries-"

"Joey!" his best friend tries to stop him from ranting on, but Joey just keeps ignoring him.

"I'm not expecting you to forgive me for what I did ... or didn't do ... and I don't expect you to care. Now if you may excuse me ..."

With that, wiping blood off his nose, Joey storms off the hospital.

"Yo, wait a sec–" Nico calls out.

"I'm alright, just ... leave me be right now–" Joey tells his best friend, not stopping.

"But-Lily's parents–"

"You take care of them for me, 'kay? I can't face them right now–" Joey's voice cracks, he stops for a while and glances over to Nico's direction. "And don't worry about me—I'll just get some fresh air."

Joey heads to his car. He gets in and starts the engine. It roars as he steps on the gas pedal. It's good to hear his car roar as he wants badly to roar and unload himself of the pain in his heart.

He drives off. To nowhere. He doesn't have any plan of route. He doesn't know where to go. He just wants to drive ... drive to where his heart leads him to.

As he gets down the dimly-lit and empty streets, as dark as the state of his heart, he wonders, Why was he left alive? Why does Lily have to die and not him? After all, he lacked enough time to spend with one of the people he held close to his heart, and when he did get time for her, she was taken away. He knows he has his shortcomings like any person but he tries to be there and make up for it. Heck, he can't even pinpoint what else he has done wrong or went wrong, but deep down, he knows it's his fault somehow.

A tear rolls down his left eye. He tries to wipe it off while driving but it keeps pouring out. Next thing he knows, he's crying a river. Everything is just too much. Everything is too painful. He wants it all to go away. And despite him wanting to scream out and sob loudly, he just keeps it all in. He's always been the type to cry quietly as a little boy. After all, why bother letting it all out when you are responsible for things you're crying about?

Then a realization hit him: would Lily be upset by all this? Wasn't she so forgiving of him? She was like Mama Mary full of unconditional love, willing to forgive and love him even when he didn't deserve it.

If she is here, she'd definitely scold me and tell me to stop thinking that way and make the most of anything and move forward, no matter how painful.

He knows he has to move on, take time in his grief, and let go of her ... but can he? Can he really let go of Lily?

All of a sudden, his train of thought is interrupted as Joey nears a converging road, and he is about to hit the wrong lane and collide with a pickup truck. He turns the wheel–but doing so causes his trunk to hit the hood of the pickup truck. His car spins and drifts uncontrollably across the street, eventually hitting a tree.

CRASH!

Joey hears the loud thud of the hood of his car as it smashes into a huge old tree. Upon impact, Joey is sent flying off from his driver's seat to the passenger's seat, his head hitting the door so hard he feels his ear explode and ring loudly.

Is this how he's going to die? How poetic. They both die because of a car crash, one after the other, on the same night. But no, even though he ruminates about wanting to die, a faint feeling of regret grows inside him. Joey doesn't want to die. He doesn't want to go out like this.

He tries to reach out for the door to open it, but his eyelids are weakening, wanting to close. He doesn't want to ... he wants to change things if only God would just allow him to do so.

In a while, he loses consciousness. *This is the end of me.* At least, that is what he is thinking of. He finds himself resting on his table in his seat, slowly opening his eyes to a foggy noise and blurry lights shining ...

"Joey? Joey? Joey!"

Chapter 4

Manic Moves, Drowsy Dreams

Joey finds himself back at the lecture room with Nico waking him up. He straightens his posture while seated.

Huh? What happened? He looks around and down at himself. What happened to his injuries? His broken leg and aching head? *All gone!*

He sees a couple of his classmates staring at him. Is this all just déjà vu? Or is it just some wild dream?

"You better be prepared for a recitation. Professor Peterson's bound to call out random blokes, especially the sleeping ones."

Those were the same words Nico said about Professor Peterson. He stares at Nico. Just then, Mr. Peterson calls him.

"Yes, Professor?" Joey stands up and asks.

The Professor then asks the same question, "In our study of ethical frameworks, we've delved into the theory of utilitarianism, which proposes that the right action is the one that maximizes overall happiness or pleasure and minimizes suffering for the greatest number of people. Can you cite a real-life scenario where utilitarian principles are applied?"

Knowing that Professor Peterson will like his answer, Joey confidently states, "Think about the ethical dilemma surrounding vaccination distribution during a pandemic." He pauses to clear his throat. "With limited doses available, utilitarianism would prioritize high-risk groups, like healthcare workers and the elderly, to save the most lives and minimize the spread of whatever sickness they must be battling in that hypothetical situation."

"Excellent answer, Mr. Barbossa." Mr. Peterson gives out a contented smile, nodding. "And with that, I believe we've covered enough ground for today. Class is dismissed."

Everyone gets up from their chairs and heads toward the doors, making footstep noise and conversation along the way.

Joey takes out and looks at his phone to check the date. *Today is still the 17th of January, at exactly twelve noon. Maybe Lily will text him this time around?*

Wait, no. Still no response.

"Aye, Joey! You good, bruv?" Nico nudges and shakes him in his seat. "Lucky that you got the answer right somehow."

Joey stays silent for a while, then looks at Nico with a slight chuckle. "Yeah, I got myself a bad dream from sleeping in class, that's all."

"Oh yeah?" Nico raises an eyebrow, adjusting his eyeglasses.

Joey nods. "For some reason ... I find myself remembering it all clearly. Too clearly even, man."

"Really?"

"Really! I first woke up in class and got called by Mr. Peterson for recitation. I asked you for love advice since Lily and I were falling out, then I headed to her place, talked it out and we went on a date ..."

"Uh huh." Nico crosses his arms, listening attentively.

Joey continues, "Then as we headed to the parking lot on the other side of the road, she got hit by a truck. I rushed her to the hospital, but she didn't make it. Her parents got mad and I had to go out for a drive. I then got into a car crash and ... here I am."

Nico nods at this, trying to process what his best friend is saying. "Yeah, you're trippin', mate," he comments, "or maybe a very surreal lucid dream, I dunno."

"Huh."

"Besides, you said you and Lily're having a bit of a falling out?" Nico asks, but doesn't wait for an answer as he continues, "well, maybe think of that dream as a reminder to make the most of being with Lily."

Joey pauses for a moment to retort, to question if he's really experiencing the same things again or he's going nuts. However, Nico has a point; it can be just a dream with his subconscious telling him to enjoy time with Lily.

"Alright," he says, now standing up with his stuff and shuffling off toward the lecture hall's exit, slinging his bag over his shoulder. "Off to lunch then!"

"Yup," Nico says with a grunt, stretching his arms out as he gets up to follow. "Wilbur's Dining?"

"Yeah," nods Joey. "Why not?"

As the day progresses, Joey finds himself going through the same experience. And now, he's on a date again with Lily.

On this second chance, rather than ruminate on what's happening, he decides to take Nico's advice: make the most of his time with Lily. He will appreciate her more on this date, from the way she sings, the way she smiles, the way she holds his arm, the way she laughs—simply everything. On this date, he will enjoy shopping with her more, even if he knows she'd pick clothes from Evereve over Rutin or Margaret O'Brien.

Joey and Lily sit by one of the tables outside Lulu's, where they wait for their Mexican food. Oh, how he can listen to her for hours and never get tired of her voice.

"So how's the song?" Lily cuts his thoughts.

"It's based on when you first fell in love with me, yeah?" he says, instead of asking.

"How did you know?" Her eyes open wide.

"Best to listen to the lyrics, right?" he replies. "The lyrics really hit me hard, babe. And I think everyone's gonna love it!"

She beams with joy. "Well, I'm ... glad you like it!"

Joey smiles. "Hey look, our food's here!" He points to the server, who puts down two styrofoam containers with plastic utensils.

The couple nod and mouth "thanks" to the server who smiles back.

As they synchronously open the food containers, Lily raises her phone to take a picture of what she's about to eat. However, with Joey sticking to his roots, he makes the sign of the cross, and she does too, and they give thanks for the food together. After that, they dig in.

"How's the food?" Joey asks with his mouth full.

Lily covers her mouth as she chews, swallowing before speaking. "It's alright," she comments. "Giving it like a six-wait, no, a seven out of ten."

"Decent rating though."

"Mhm." She goes on to chow down her Beef Fajitas with a fork. They are silent for a while as they eat when she suddenly blurts out, "Whoever finishes their food last, owes fifty bucks!"

"Huh?" Joey's jaw drops in shock.

Well, it isn't really that shocking. He knows she is going to pull something like this, but hey, whatever gets her giggling. With that, both get back to eating, attempting to finish their meal first.

"I'm full, could you have all of this instead?" she asks with puppy eyes, handing over her meal. She only has a quarter portion of her fajitas left.

"Oh yeah?" He raises an eyebrow. "You serious?"

"Yes. I can't finish everything ..." she answers, pouting.

Joey is skeptical at first, but willingly eats her portion of the food even if he hasn't finished his yet.

"HAHAHAHA! I WIN!" she bursts out laughing. "Now you owe me fifty!"

Looking at just how much she's enjoying herself, Joey doesn't complain on her cheating her way out of the challenge. He's just happy to hear that sweet laugh of hers.

"Soooo, got anywhere else you wanna go?" he asks and stops laughing.

"I have a group project tomorrow and I gotta get up early so no." Lily shakes her head.

"You really wanna head back home now?" He feels nervous. To mask it, he opens his water bottle, downing every single drop, and closes the bottle.

"Yeah, and next time, I'll be the one taking you out on a date!"

"Whatever you say, princess." Joey nods, getting up and holding the shopping bags for her. He waits for her to stand up and they walk off, with Lily holding onto his arm.

Joey throws the water bottles into a trash bin on the way out. They walk on until they are by the pedestrian near the intersection.

As they cross the road, he hears a familiar noise, recognizes the beeping and screeching of tires from an incoming truck coming their way. Something clicks in his mind. Time seems to slowly crawl as Joey's mind races, realizing that he's been here before. The story he told Nico isn't a dream or a trippy déjà vu. It is all real.

Could he be stuck in a time loop and now reliving the same scenes over? If this is the case, maybe, he can do something. He can change their fate. He can save Lily.

Before Lily can react, Joey's instincts take over, his arms wrap around her protectively as they tumble to the safety of the sidewalk. They roll onto the sidewalk, narrowly dodging the truck that could've crushed them. It leaves them breathless and shaken. Thank God they're alive. Thank God, Lily's alive!

But then, without warning, something unexpected happens. A sedan comes through, its driver's vision obscured by the aftermath of the truck's crash, hurtles toward them with terrifying speed. Realizing there's no time to escape, Joey closes his eyes shut as he shields Lily with his own body, bracing for the inevitable impact.

WHAM!

He feels the car's bone-jarring force slamming into them, and he lets out a blood-curdling scream in pain.

He opens his eyes and realizes that he's back at the lecture hall at twelve noon of January 17th.

"AGH!" Joey jolts backwards, causing him to fall off his seat and hit the floor with an echoing THUD! The young man looks around, dazed and confused as he pats every part of his body that should've been broken by the car crash.

"Blimey!" Nico screeches in shock, recoiling back. "Whatchu dreaming about, mate?"

Joey grunts as he regains his balance and sits back up. "I know what you're about to say. That Mr. Peterson will call us for a recitation-" he adds frantically, "plus, he's gonna call me a few seconds from now. And I know his question, and I have an answer for it."

"Huh? How did you know all that?" asks Nico, weirded out by all of this.

"*Final Destination* type of premonition, I guess."

Meanwhile, the Professor notices Joey's yelping, eyeing him from where he is at. "You okay there, Mr. Barbossa?"

"I'm good, Professor–" Joey then stands up, his hand on his aching lower back. "Got a question for me, Sir?"

"As a matter of fact, yes." Mr. Peterson clears his throat.

Nico's face seems to be asking, "What in the world is going on?"

"In our study of ethical frameworks," Mr. Peterson says, "we've delved into the theory of utilitarianism—"

But of course, Joey doesn't have to listen because he already knows the question.

"See? Told you." Joey leans in and whispers to Nico before answering the question.

"Think of a hypothetical situation surrounding vaccination distribution during a pandemic," Joey begins and delivers the rest of his answer.

"Excellent answer, Mr. Barbossa." Mr. Peterson nods and gives a contented smile. "And with that, I believe we've covered enough ground for today. Class is dismissed."

With that, everyone in the lecture hall begins flocking out, leaving Joey and Nico behind.

"So, do you believe me?" asks Joey. "And the fact that I could be some time traveler or whatever?"

"It's more like *Groundhog Day* to me by the way you're predicting everything," Nico replies. "But yeah, I believe you."

Joey then sighs with relief, combing back his curly hair. "Thank God."

"You know you probably won't believe this but my uncle and grandma are time travelers too, if you'd call it that."

"Huh? Could you tell me more 'bout this?"

"You bet!" Nico smirks as he walks to the blackboard, grabbing a chalk.

Joey would like to understand what he's going through and find a way to save Lily.

Chapter 5

Looking for Love When the Climate is Cold

The lecture on the phenomenon that Joey is experiencing begins as Nico draws on the blackboard; the chalk scrapes the surface with him drawing an arrow.

"This signifies your life," Nico says as he taps on the sharp end of the drawn arrow. The flow of your life or the flow of time. Let's label it 'FLOW'." And Nico labels it with big letters.

"Handwriting's terrible as always but okay," Joey mumbles as he nods, his hand rubbing his chin as he concentrates on the figure.

"Oh, shut yo' mouth! Anyways." Nico makes a swirling scribble on the end of the arrow, labeling it "TRIGGERS". "This thing represents triggers. There are two kinds of triggers: motivational and physical."

"What's the difference between the two of them?" Joey furrows his eyebrows.

Nico explains, "Well, motivational triggers are the emotions and the traumatic events that drive you to go to a time loop, whereas physical triggers are the rituals you do to get yourself to the time loop. They always work together to make you go back in time–"

"How come you know about this?"

"Told you, it's in the family. So we, the next generation, might have the gift too. So, grandma thought it best to make sure we know about it."

"How about some examples then?" Joey interrupts.

"How did you get yourself in this mess anyways?"

"I remember I was first in a car crash, and then I went back again from another car crash," says Joey.

Playfully, he points a finger gun at Joey. "That is your main physical trigger: knocked unconscious or at death's door. And what about the messed up shtick that happened to you?"

"Lily ..." Joey hesitates for a minute. "Died while we were on a date."

Nico pauses for a while, gulping and nodding with understanding. "Good grief," he mutters and pauses before asking, "can we now move on to loops?"

He then draws a curved arrow upward, curving down and pointing to the start of the FLOW arrow. He labels it "LOOP".

"A loop is where you go back to the start of the day of the traumatic event and into the FLOW. Like, say for example, my grandma lost her pet cat. She went to sleep, feeling guilty for losing the cat and that got her back in time. We call this 'The Art of Time Looping'!"

Then he writes "TIME LOOPING" with two lines underneath to emphasize it. "It's how Phil Conners from *Groundhog Day* gets himself into a loop over and over and over again."

Nico then faces Joey dead in the eye. "Here's the thing about time looping: if you change something within the flow as you loop in time, the flow will find a way to cover up that change."

Upon hearing this, Joey's heart begins to sink down to his gut. "So that explains the loop ..."

"Yeah," Nico nods.

"Is there a way that we can go around it?" Joey asks the most important question of all. "So I can save Lily?"

Nico is taken aback, sighing. "You don't, Joey," he says somberly. "I'm sorry."

"But I can't just let her go like that, man, I-" Joey's voice is barely above a whisper. "Are you saying that we should let her be just like that?"

"My uncle not only got his legs blown off by a landmine during the war in Iran, he also couldn't prevent a divorce. Guess what? He didn't find a way to avoid it," Nico says sternly, staring down into Joey's soul. "It drove him INSANE, Joey."

"What's insane is that you're going to let Lily die because of some bogus time looping!" Joey shouts, standing up from his seat and marching angrily toward Nico.

"It's not bogus, you're literally experiencing it right now!" Nico shouts back, but tries to bite his tongue and not lash out.

"There's gotta be a way to save her!" Joey is agitated now, grabbing his friend by the collar with all his might. "Tell me, there's a way to save Lily!"

"Even if you find a way, you'll just make things worse!" Nico loses his temper completely, pushing down Joey's hands off him. "With you out here trying to save her over and over again—you're just creating your own personal freaking hell, bruv!"

"Don't worry about me, Nico. What we should worry about is Lily!"

"Why shouldn't I worry about you? I was in love with Lily one time but she dumped me. I still care about her as a friend, so don't you dare accuse me of being heartless. You got me!" Nico croaks out, hurt by what Joey said. "I mean, why are we even arguing about this? Why even come to me about this to begin with?"

Then the guilt hits Joey like a freight train. Oh what a horrible friend he is! If he goes on trying to save Lily so badly, he might lose Nico. He can't handle losing two people closest to him. He is his first friend in America, Joey does care, but at the same time, he just can't give up Lily.

And so, he is adamant in finding ways to save his beloved. He shakes his head and walks out with his stuff, leaving Nico alone in the lecture hall.

The young man decides from that point on to keep his plan of saving Lily to himself. He will not bother telling Nico how his loops go. And so, the time traveler positions himself to jump into the past.

However, despite his efforts, Lily is still dying. In the next loop, a car crashes onto a pedestrian lamp post, it breaks, falls over, crushing her. In another one, Joey gets himself and Lily evade the truck, the car spinning in their direction, and the pedestrian pole falling over them. However, amid the chaos, a car hits one of the electrical boxes nearby, causing it to explode. Both of them get caught in the explosion, bringing him to the next loop.

As Joey wakes up from the latest loop, Nico tells him to let things be the way they are to stop the loop.

At this point, Nico is getting more and more impatient, angry and upset with him.

But Joey is stubborn. *There is a way to get out of the time loops AND to save Lily. I can do it.*

This leads to another loop ...

And another ...

And another ...

And another ...

Until it has taken a toll on him.

Nico seems right all along. This crusade to fight for Lily's life is destroying him. He can't bear holding up like this over and over. He has had enough but even then, still keeps going like a madman. And yet, the argument he had with the long past version of Nico has stuck with him.

"Whoever finishes their food last owes fifty bucks!" Lily exclaims as she chows down on her Beef Fajitas.

However, Joey finds himself zoning out, simply staring blankly at his Chicken Fajitas. Even on his date with Lily, Joey is distraught by what he has done to Nico.

"Are you okay, Joey?" Lily asks. She stops eating for a while as she places her hand over his.

"Oh, uh-" exclaims Joey as he gets back to his senses. "Nothing, sorry for zoning out."

Lily doesn't buy it. She frowns and crosses her arms. It's her way of saying, just spill the beans.

It sure gets him talking. "Me and Nico ... got into an argument."

"What?" She frowns even more. "What happened?"

Joey ponders on what to say next. He knows that by talking about their argument, he's about to reveal himself as a time looper. However, he isn't sure if he must even tell her. Should he or should he not?

"Joey," Lily says calmly, looking deeply into his eyes, "you can tell me anything."

With an exhale and Lily's soothing voice, the words just slip out of his tongue. "You ... were supposed to die in a car accident. Then I found myself in a time loop, and I kept going back to save you. But it's not working. I keep losing you. Nico keeps telling me to stop saving you. But I can't just let you ..." He couldn't say the word "die".

Lily is astounded, speechless.

A sigh exits Joey's mouth; he shakes his head as he opens his plastic bottle and gulps some water. "I don't know what to do. All I know is I want to save you."

"You're a time loop-er?" Lily asks.

"Time looper, yeah, I guess." Joey nods.

Lily freezes and hesitates to speak. Why is she hesitant? Is she hiding something?

"You see ..." she finally speaks, her tone stern as her eyes pierces his. "I'm a time looper too."

Chapter 6

Soul Alone, Soul Really Matters to Me

Joey laughs nervously. "Wait, what?" he asks.

He must've misheard it. It can't be.

"That's right," Lily says with a heavy voice and hangs her head low. "I guess this is what I am ... what we are ... I'm a time looper like you."

This time, it's Joey who is at a loss for words as his mind races. *Lily is a time looper? Since when? Why didn't she tell me? She acts pretty much the same all throughout the loops, unlike Nico.*

"I know what you're thinking, Joey. How did I even become a time looper like you?"

Joey is quiet and watches his beloved.

She clears her throat. "It happened when I was little. About twice. And when you tried to save me I woke up in my bedroom, then you came in and we went on a date. Then I die again. Each time, each loop- I just ... died. You go out of your way to save me, but each time, it just goes wrong."

Joey shakes his head, feeling his heart breaking apart. "Why didn't you tell me?"

"I thought it's all just me ... Joey, look at me." She looks at him lovingly. "Please stop saving me. Please."

"Stop saving you?" Joey is in disbelief; his voice, strained. "But ... I can't just stand by and watch you ... die, Lily. I can't-"

"You don't get it, do you? I'm supposed to die!" Her voice is filled with frustration. "Besides, what if these trucks and poles and whatnot crush other people because I didn't die?"

Joey pleads, choking in his own emotions, "Don't say it like that, Lily! Please-"

"Stop it, Joey! Don't play God." Lily rises from her seat, grabs her handbag, and makes her way toward the exit without a second glance.

Joey gets up and runs to catch up with her. "Hey, wait!"

Lily quickens her pace and sprints. She doesn't even wait for the pedestrian traffic lights to go from red to green. And when the traffic lights change color, Joey instantly knows something bad will happen.

"LILY!" he calls out, his voice hoarse with desperation.

A fast truck comes and its driver seems frantic. It looks like the truck has no brakes and will crash on anything on its path. Joey runs, tackling Lily out of the truck's way, getting them onto the sidewalk, with Joey landing on his back and Lily on top of her boyfriend.

Suddenly, the truck hits a nearby car so hard it spins around and about to hit the two. Quickly predicting this, he drags Lily out of the truck's way and that of the lamp post that is about to fall on them. As they run out to the open parking lot, they hear an explosion ring out from the electric boxes by the traffic light post.

"This is what I meant by everything going wrong as long as I'm still alive!" Lily yells as she tries to run off, but Joey is holding her tight by the wrist. "Let go of me!"

"I can't, Lily!" Joey cries out, not letting go. "I've done too much to stop, okay?"

"I never asked you to save me!" Lily sobs, tears running down her face. "It hurts seeing you doing so much like this ... all for me!"

"I just want to keep you safe–"

"Not when you're hurting yourself because of it, you selfish jerk!"

"Do I have to die to keep you alive?" Joey asks frustratingly. "What if I die right now?"

"Please don't, Joey!" she pleads, "please!"

Then all of the sudden, Lily clutches her chest, looking as if her chest is feeling tight, spasming with pain.

"Lily!" Joey cries out, his voice filled with desperation and horror. He drops to his knees beside her as the sound of sirens wailing blast to his ears. "No, no, no ... stay with me, please ..."

"Joey," she whispers, too weak to speak. "If you really love me, you ... should let ... me go and ... be happy."

She loses consciousness, the life of her blue eyes fading away as she closes them, her body limp, heavy and cold, as Joey carries her in his arms. He has seen her deaths a lot of times but seeing her like this as he holds her close ... it breaks his already broken heart into a million pieces.

At this point, he realizes that Nico is right. So right, even Lily is on it. He should just let her go. By trying to save her, he made her go through a lot of deaths.

As paramedics see Joey hold Lily's limp body, they rush over and carry her on a stretcher. Seeing Lily sent off to the hospital in an ambulance, Joey makes his way back to his car and sinks into the driver's seat, the leather upholstery cold against his skin. He sits there, his thoughts swirling in a tumultuous whirlwind of anguish and despair.

Finally, with a heavy heart, Joey starts the engine and pulls out of the parking lot. The car zooms off into the night. He is just dazed and out of his mind, staring into nothingness as he drives, with not much attention to what's in front of him.

As Joey drives, he sees them: a mother and child walking along the sidewalk, illuminated by the soft glow of streetlights. He realizes he is moving too fast and swerves to stay clear of them, but it is too late.

A loud CRASH fills the air as the automobile hits the nearby tree, making him lose consciousness.

Chapter 7

You're Out of Touch, I'm Out of Time

Joey is going through another loop—the last time he'll see Lily alive. He knows he has to make the most of the time he has left with her. No, it isn't that he has to, he WANTS to. He wants to cherish every moment.

However, something just isn't sitting right. It feels off. He feels like something is amiss, that a gaping hole is sucking out his joy and excitement. The same joy and excitement he had back when he was going on dates with Lily are gone. He feels empty.

And why not, when he is faced with the death of a lover over and over in time loops? It just leaves him questioning everything. Like, why bother being stuck in the same day on repeat? Why bother going back in time again and again if you can't change its outcome? What is the point? Why should he go on like this?

"Whoever finishes their food last owes fifty bucks!" Lily exclaims, now munching on her order.

Joey snaps out of zoning off and daydreaming, faking a smile as he too eats his Mexican food.

"Are you okay, Joey?" she asks. She must've noticed how off he is today.

"Of course!" He nods, forcing a smile. "Why do you ask?"

Lily raises an eyebrow. "I can't ask if my boyfriend is alright?"

"It's alright, just wondering why you're pretending that you didn't ask to be saved."

"Then what? You're gonna guard me my whole life so that I won't die horribly?"

"Will it be selfish if I want to just have you even for a little longer, Lily?" Joey answers coldly. "I've just come to terms with the fact that you'll die, anyways."

This catches Lily by surprise, leaving her silent. It is still the same Lily back at the last loop. Joey, seeing her Beef Fajitas with only around one fourth left, takes it and eats it.

Awkward silence lingers on their table. After a while, Joey speaks up again, "Also–"

"Hm?" Lily raises both her eyebrows.

"May I at least drive you home?" he asks, pausing as he opens a bottle of water, chugs all the water down, then closes it before continuing, "even if it means for the last time?"

Lily says nothing. She simply nods and they both stand up and grab their stuff. They walk out of Lulu's towards the sidewalk, to the pedestrian lane. They wait for the pedestrian traffic lights to turn green before crossing. As they cross the road, Joey notices that there is no truck or car to run them over, no traffic light poles to crush them, and no electric boxes exploding.

Just what is going on? Is this God letting them go easily? He thinks.

He has no clue.

Reaching his car, he ushers Lily inside before getting in, starting the engine and driving off, heading to Lily's place. Everything is quiet except for the radio playing "Car's Outside" by James Arthur and Joey humming along.

They park at Mirrielees, just a stone's throw away from her place. They head out and cross a street and walk up to Lily's door.

Lily stares at the door, her hand getting inches closer to the handle. However, she stops and turns around to Joey. Her eyes well up with tears. She tries to say something but no words come out. At that point, she sobs. Immediately, Joey hugs her tightly, his arms around her.

"I don't wanna go, Joey!" cries Lily, "I should've texted you right away, sent you good morning and good evening texts! I shouldn't have spent too much time with music! I'm sorry, Joey—I don't wanna leave like this!"

"You won't be leaving," says Joey, putting his hand on her cheek, "since you're always gonna be here with me." He touches his heart.

"You're so cheesy." She laughs sadly as she sniffles. "I hate you."

"And I love you too." Joey smiles as both of them lean for a tender kiss, their eyes closed to feel the moment.

Eventually, they pull away, both smiling now.

"Good night, pookie bear," Lily says, wiping the tears off her eyes, laughing a bit at his pet name.

"Good night, little miss," Joey replies as a bittersweet smile forms on his face, teary-eyed.

Both step away after saying their farewells—the young woman walks in while the young man walks out of the building.

What's dreadful about goodbyes like this is that even if you know that you'll never see, never hear, and never touch them again, you know that their voice, their laughter, their face, and their touch will be etched in your memory. And it hurts.

Back at Mirrielees, Joey sees Nico getting ready for bed.

It's obviously not the same Nico from the last loop whom he argued with about not saving Lily. But at the same time, Joey feels guilty for hurting him. He already held back tears when he had to let go of Lily and now, he has to hold back more tears with his best friend whom he hurt.

But Joey can't hold it in anymore. His eyes are now overflowing with tears, rolling down his cheeks. Nico turns around and takes notice of this, puzzled yet concerned.

"You good, bruv?"

"No." The young man shakes his head as he quietly sobs now. "I'm not okay, man."

Knowing well what his best friend is going through, without a word, Nico approaches him and hugs him, and Joey sobs and sobs until there are no more tears to shed.

Chapter 8

I'm Out of My Head When You're Not Around

It has been three days since Lily's death. It being a rollercoaster of an experience for Joey is an understatement. All of those time loops, repeating on the same day and ending with the same fate. Now, it's over. And there is nothing he can do anymore.

The day of Lily's funeral is gray and somber, matching Joey's heavy heart as he stands outside the church, surrounded by mourners. The air is thick with grief, and Joey feels a lump form in his throat as he gazes at the sea of faces gathered to pay their respects.

He looks around, seeing everyone in black and white clothes like him. There are those whom he doesn't recognize like Lily's relatives, those whom he doesn't know that much like Jessica, Lily's roommate, and those who know her the most.

Firstly, there are Mr. and Mrs. Forester, Lily's parents, seated at Joey's right, the strain in their eyes showing, the weight of their loss heavy upon them as they greet mourners with forced smiles. After several apologies, they realized that Joey was not to blame for their daughter's death.

Next, there is Lily's old friend, Nico, who is bawling, unable to finish his eulogy and now is ushering in Joey to speak.

Right after giving Nico a bro hug, Joey walks up to the podium, pausing to gather his thoughts and what he wants to say before putting the microphone near his mouth.

"I never was the kind to get into a relationship. As a scholar at Stanford, my intention of moving from the Philippines to the US was to study. Getting into a relationship was not part of the plan, especially not in my freshman year. What I didn't know was that someone would come crashing in, changing the course of my life ... Lilian Forester.

Lily was one of a kind. A wonderful person, very talented and kind. To me, she was everything."

Joey pauses as he chokes in tears. His eyes well up, but he holds it in and keeps his composure.

"I loved her very much, but I ... I feel awful that I didn't get to say it enough. I showed it more with my actions usually but there's just some things words can *do* instead of our actions. It affects us way more than a punch or kick would.

When she died, I thought that if I did something differently, maybe she'd be here and we won't be having a funeral. I know now that there's nothing I can do about it, but it's okay. I know she'll be happy when we've happily moved on. The only bare minimum she'll want is to be remembered."

A melancholic yet hopeful feeling comes over Joey as he finishes his speech and steps down the podium. But his thoughts continue to linger on his beloved Lily. Her smile, her laughter, her voice, her memories. His experiences with her, good or bad, will always be precious to him.

Acknowledgment

Writing a book is amazing but it is never about going solo. That is why there are numerous people whom I want to thank.

Firstly, I want to thank God for bestowing me the gift of writing and urge me to use said gift of writing to showcase for everyone to see. I haven't known what my purpose is for the last few years and now I am actually publishing this to the world to read.

I want to thank Ms. Refime Amor and Ms. Rhoda Osalvo, my editor and my teacher at the Book Writers Club Batch 5, respectively. Both of them guided me and assisted me in crafting this very first book of mine. Both of them were very intrigued by my idea when I pitched it initially. I knew for a fact that this was rough around the edges but without them, this would have been a mess.

They say don't judge a book by its cover. It certainly isn't the case when a book cover is one of the things needed to draw the reader's attention. With this, I'd also like to thank James Irwin Esparas, the artist behind the magnificent artwork for the book cover and the illustrations in between pages. When I first saw his version of the book cover, I was blown away and found it much more refined and amazing compared to what I made.

Next up, I'd also like to especially thank my friend and fellow author at BWC, A.J. Antonio, for helping me out with my writing. He recommended some ideas for my book to make things interesting as well as gave some writing advice. Though some suggestions were scrapped during development, I took his idea of not making Lily just a character meant to be fridged. Fun fact: we are also in The Writers Club (different from BWC but managed by Ms. Rhoda too) and from the homeworks we're given, the way he writes is just outstanding and feels immersive. It's as if he's a professional at it and he's younger than me by a year, mind you. I think this is also a good segue to recommend reading his book, "Guts and Grit."

To one collaborator and friend of mine, I'd like to also give special thanks to Gab Liwag. She's an upcoming music artist who's also making a song based off this book of mine. It was unexpected but a fun collaboration since we cooked up a lot when it comes to one of her songs. Also, if you're reading this Gab, you're actually an inspiration for Lily, a character in this story, mostly basing off the music artist stuff since I didn't really plan out what career the character has in the story. Make sure to check out her socials at @RIELLA on Spotify and @ri.e.lla on Instagram.

Without readers, a book would be useless. Thus, I'd like to thank my Beta Readers, who are anonymous to me until this day. Whoever you may be, thank you for giving me feedback and enjoying the early stages of the manuscript.

To my friends out there, wanting to get this book pre-ordered, thank you too for your support. Hope you understand that the reason I haven't been going out and hanging out much is because of this book.

To my family, who helped me publish this book and supported my dreams to publish a book—without you guys, I can't pursue this milestone.

Finally, there's you, my readers who went out their way to buy and read this. Writing "Out of Touch, Out of Time" was a blast for me. I hope you may have learned something and I hope you are inspired by this one way or another. Thank you all from the bottom of my heart.

Because of this writing and publishing experience which I found fun, I plan on making more books like this in the future. Until then, stay tuned and see you in the next project!

About the Author

Johnny Boneo is just your typical guy with a wide imagination and nerdy interest in all things lore and fiction. He is a Grade 11 homeschooler at CFA Freedom. "Out of Touch, Out of Time" is his debut book.

Book Writers Club
Batch 5

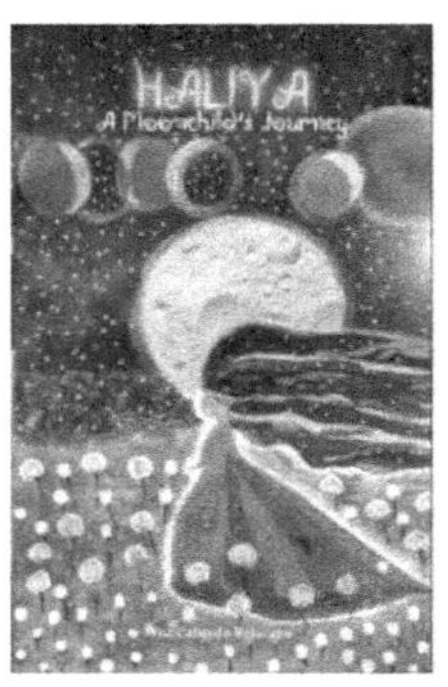

Haliya:
A Moonchild's Journey
by Yna Cabredo Balacano

Magayon:
A Tale of Childhood,
Friendship, and Courage
by Yva Cabredo Balacano

Charlie
by Gayle Robrigado

Ghosting You
by Luna Paulo

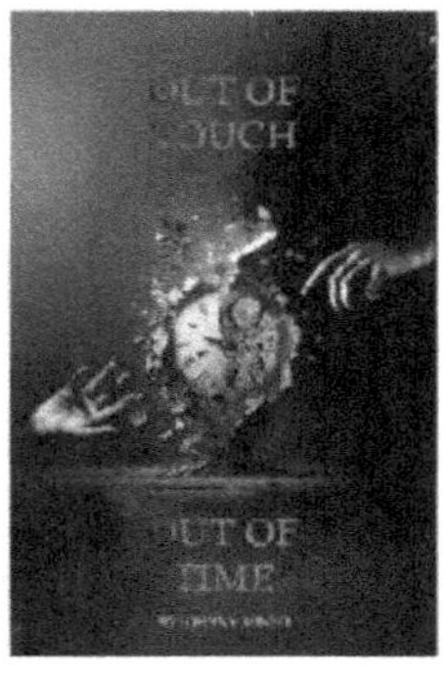

Out of Touch,
Out of Time
by Johnny Boneo

Guts and Grit
by A.J. Antonio

Other Titles from the Book Writers Club

Temporarily Vanilla by Kiersten Cheryl Abadicio

Ori by Kiersten Abadicio

The Other Way Around by Phoebe Adorza

Vehemence by Prince Gabriel M. Adorza

The 7th by Manu Aguilar

The Tale of the Morning People by Chayylielle Antazo

Rey Collins and the Beast Within by X.G. Antazo

Rey Collins and the Stag of Leighis by X.G. Antazo

Two Hours Before Midnight by Lexie Bautista

A Little Boy's Promise by Mabbi Bautista

Homeschooled in the Kitchen by Pio Calungcaguin

Simple Joys: 4 Stories to Read on a Rainy Day by Jillian Canapi

Silverson by Pio Fetizanan

The Zombie Invasion by Miguel Jeremy

Asho: The Boy who Saved the World by Arl Kanapi

The Dark Princess by Jannah Brielle Lising

Surf the Skies by Emman Lorenzo

One Summer in Bert's LIfe by Miguel Lorenzo

The Girl with the Gift by Bettina Reika A. Namoco

The Last Page by Bianca Ofreneo

Boundary Break: To Far and Beyond by Erl Rozwald F. Raba

Crystal Quest by Hans Karlo Salaria

Brinderbrook Spies by Nikita Santos

The Birtwick Files by Nikita Santos

To get updates, visit our Facebook page:

https://www.facebook.com/bookwritersclub123

To get a copy of our books, email:
bookwritersclub123@gmail.com

Or search the title and author on Amazon.com.

www.ingramcontent.com/pod-product-compliance
Lightning Source LLC
LaVergne TN
LVHW050333160826
845677LV00014B/3614

* 9 7 8 6 2 1 0 6 1 4 5 2 7 *